TITLE

The Gross Rose

By Sidra Mohsin

Chapter 1

"Beaustaf family." The noisy host broadcast to the a huge number of individuals in the room just as the family in a fixed region. "For your wrongdoings and treachery against His Majesty, Roderick, you have been condemned to death by the virus fingers of the void of room. Spread the word about it, this day in will stand out forever as the day that the administration of President Beaustaf has finished. Long live King Roderick!"

A cheer emitted once he squeezed a button opening the room the family was in to the vacuum of room. That was the first of numerous passings on the Ashaton space make.

The Ashaton was a specialty worked for individuals of Earth to leave on life in space. After the number of inhabitants in Earth had developed past the rate the globe could deal with, 1.3 billion residents of world passed on the blue and green planet to look for life past the stars. That was back in 2153 AD. It is as of now 2547 AD. I was there that day. The day the transformation started.

My dearest companion remained at the top of the remainder of the watchman and looked as these honest individuals were killed. I chose without even a moment's pause I would not represent this. Since that day, I have counted 846 extra passings as a result of the conspiracy the new lord accepted these individuals submitted. However, I realized that these individuals did nothing of the sort. This upheaval would end, and I would be the one to end it.

I turned into the Blue Rose.

A year had passed since that day the President and his family were killed. Since that day, things between my closest companion, Jered, and I had become rough. I didn't uphold this upheaval while he was the right hand man to Roderick. I was doing all that I could to avoid Roderick's grip while attempting to help individuals, however the interaction was slow. I expected to change my methodology.

Before I turned into the Blue Rose, I was basically attempting to find data on individuals that would require help stowing away, however I had very little to continue and essentially wasn't having an effect. I frequently didn't find who required assistance until it was past the point of no return. I needed to adopt a more actual strategy to the issue.

I recalled at the time an old story, a work of art, that many individuals cherished during our lifespan. It had been to some degree failed to remember when we headed out to the stars. The Scarlet Pimpernel recounted the narrative of an upheaval similar as our own, and a man who had the option to trick a huge gathering of individuals to thinking he was a numbskull while he saved many individuals from a killing machine called the Guillotine.

Many focuses in the story resembled my own present life and I realized I needed to turn into exactly the same thing as Sir Percival Blakeney. I needed to turn into my own Pimpernel.

To start with, I should have been ready to ensure myself. I fortunately made them train with good reason. In any case, to give myself an edge, I concentrated on methodology and various strategies utilized in wars, unrests, and various fights. I before long turned out to be exceptionally solid in strategical plans, and surprisingly worked everything out such that few companions wouldn't play specific games with me.

The troublesome aspect of the entire thing was getting the data I should have been ready to save these individuals. My most obvious opportunity was with Jered, yet I would have rather not maneuver anybody into this with me. On the off chance that any life must be lost in saving these individuals, I just needed it to be mine.

During the time I was attempting to sort out what to do in the present circumstance, a thump came at my entryway. I stood up and addressed the entryway. Fortunately, the greater part of my arrangements had been covered up in light of the fact that Jered was at my entryway.

"Jered." I expressed in shock.

He peered down at me with miserable eyes. "Hitomi, we really want to talk."

My chest hurt, however I didn't uphold his inclusion with Roderick. "I thought I said all I expected to a year prior when this all began."

"However, I don't think you comprehend my expectations." He tossed back at me. "I'm simply doing what I can to remain alive."

"Furthermore, the most ideal way is by favoring the despot?"

"Hitomi..."

Tears began to frame in my eyes. Tears I thought were evaporated. "You broke your guarantee the second you consented to work with Roderick."

"Please, Hitomi." he asked. "I simply need a companion at the present time."

His eyes showed that he had seen a great deal that day and genuinely required another person around. I wavered yet made the way for him and permitted him into my room. He gradually strolled in and plunked down on the little love seat I had. His head naturally fell into his hands, and his shoulders started to shake. I sat next to him and put an arm around his wide structure and scoured his arm with my other hand.

"You don't have a clue that it is so difficult to see families killed ordinary." He said in the middle of cries. "Today was a little group of three. They just had a child young lady. That youngster never at any point got to encounter life prior to being tossed to the vacuum of room."

My heart jumped with torment. One more three lives to be added to the individuals who were unreasonably killed for the fulfillment of a despot. Jered wasn't done at this point.

"He intends to take another family that actually trusts in popular government." He quieted a few. "Tomorrow is a group of five that he intends to kill at fourteen ticks. This one will be at the port side sealed area."

He gazed toward me. "I realize you disdain it, however will you be there?"

I wanted this data. Knowing the time and where worked everything out such that I could save them. I simply required an arrangement.

"I'll be there." I told him.

'Despite the fact that it may not stand out you are thinking.' I contemplated internally.

After some additional time elapsed, Jered left and I began my arrangements. I would have rather not be perceived, so I set up a basic uniform to conceal my face. It wasn't awesome, yet it worked for what I wanted.

I went through the majority of the late evening arranging my course and what explicitly I expected to do. I got my required things and set them in my pockets and on my belt. I anticipated the best and more awful of the circumstance, seeing this was my first time endeavoring to save these lives.

Light came, and it was the ideal opportunity for me to act.

Chapter 2

I needed to say something. Normally, what I would plan would be something some time before the execution done so that the casualties would be far away before they were near their chosen passings. In any case, I needed to do something else to show that there were individuals who were against this upheaval for a fake lord.

I was sitting tight for the perfect second. Taking some time before fourteen ticks to work with a portion of the electrical machines that would be utilized. Then, at that point, I paused. I was concealed inside the sealed area chamber. In any case, what a great many people didn't know was that there was a crisis get away from bring forth in the corner for cases that an individual was secured.

I looked as the family was hauled into the room, the ladies having tears in their eyes. Every one of them shuddered in dread as their lives were reaching a troublesome conclusion. My blood bubbled at seeing the supporters of Roderick reviling and spitting at these individuals.

The entryway shut and the family was secured. The speaker snapped as the host conversed with the family.

"Rembrant family!" he said in a sensational tone. "For your conspiracy against Lord Roderick, you have been condemned to death by the vacuum of room. May God show leniency toward your spirits."

That was my prompt. I squeezed the button on my remote, making the whole region go dull. The sound of shouts and yells came from the speaker and the host attempted to keep everybody quiet. I had around five minutes before the back up lights came on.

I went to the family and tenderly contacted one of their arms. "Follow me."

The mother was breathing intensely. "Who right?"

"A companion." I directed them to the incubate. "Go in here and follow the passage until the end. Avoid sight. I'll go along with you in a second."

They adhered to my directions and I shut the incubate behind them. 'This arrangement will just work once.' I contemplated internally. When the progressives learned of the incubate they would doubtlessly seal them so this wouldn't occur once more.

I stood where the Rembrant family used to be and trusted that the lights will come on. A blaze and sight got back to everybody. They investigated the sealed area unit and panted in shock. The family was mysteriously absent, and all that was there was me. Out of the countenances there, I perceived two, Jered and Roderick.

I looked as Roderick strolled over in a fury and squeezed the button that would open the external way to space. Quiet. Nothing occurred. He squeezed the button strongly a few additional occasions and was disillusioned in the result. I had concentrated on the frameworks a long time before this arrangement and detached the wire associating the button and the entryway.

I gazed Roderick in the eyes and gave a two finger showed respect for wave prior to squeezing one more button on my remote making the chamber go dim once more. With that I left the region through a similar incubate and rushed to meet with individuals I had saved.

"This unit will return you to Earth." I said as I entered the required data to the framework. "It will take you around 5 years to make it back, so you should went into cryo rest."

I went to the family, cover off and agreeable. I could see the alleviation in their eyes. They entered the unit and started to get into their chambers before cryo rest.

"How might we at any point thank you?" One man of his word asked me.

I gave him a genuine grin. "Continue to live."

I started to separately help them each into rest, setting them up for a long excursion. However, one youngster was reluctant.

I put a hand on his shoulder, his earthy colored eyes went to the ground. "What's going on?"

"I would rather not go." He said before his head gobbled up to take a gander at me. "I need to remain and help you."

"That is just plain dumb." I clarified. "I'm placing myself in extraordinary peril by doing this. I just saved you from death, I would rather not put you in another circumstance that could cause it. Moreover, you should be with your family."

"They aren't my family." He peered down once more. "My family was one of the first to be killed, I incidentally turned out to be with Tom and Sally Rembrant's family during the time. They concealed me for a year before this occurred. I need to respect my family by saving these individuals like you."

My eyebrows went up in concern. "Bud, it would be best for you to return to Earth. I would rather not put any other individual in peril along these lines."

"In any case, I can help you far beyond in case you were separated from everyone else." He contended. "I have abilities that could be useful."

'He won't take no for a reply.' I thought.

"What's your name?" I inquired.

"Jesse."

I grinned. "Indeed, Jesse. I figure we should track down a preferable spot of tasks over my room."

His eyes started to shine with happiness. "I know a spot that is huge and gives us all we really want! It's in the lower spaces of the boat too. Scarcely anybody goes there."

"You should comprehend." I clarified further. "You will not actually have the option to leave that region. You are a needed man and they will make a move to kill you."

"I will do anything to benefit these individuals." Jesse guaranteed.

I collapsed my arms. "Anyway, Jesse, what are these abilities you are so glad for?"

His smile broadened. "I'm a specialist with PC frameworks."

Chapter 3

A day had passed since the Rembrant family had left and Jesse had join my motivation. I had made my space and moved the things to the lower part of the boat, where we would set our activities. Jesse had made himself agreeable and was dealing with rebooting an unwanted PC console. He was chipping away at associating it to the Ashaton's framework, that way he could have eyes all over.

I returned the room, grabbing his eye. He turned upward from the equipment and let out a moan. "I don't have a clue, Hitomi, I'm bad with the actual machines. Programming is more my claim to fame. However, I know a person who is incredible with this stuff."

"I would rather not pull any other individual into this." I clarified. "I'm facing a major challenge simply keeping you around."

He looked irritated. "That was my decision. I feel that I will do more prominent great halting this ridiculous unrest as opposed to attempt to proceed with a typical life on the planet."

I thought briefly. "How would you realize this person will not sell us out to Roderick?"

He grinned at my inquiry. "Since he has been secluded from everything for supporting against Roderick and his upset."

"In case he's secluded from everything," I verbally processed, with a hand on my jawline. "How would we find him?"

"I know where he is." Jesse reported. "He's stowing away in these lower regions also. I can go get him and bring him here. I guarantee I will not be seen."

I didn't care for it, however I hesitantly concurred. Just before he was going to leave, I got a call. Jesse stopped to perceive what data might come from it. I checked out my wrist and saw it was from Jered. Gnawing my lip, I replied and a little holographic picture of him showed up on my wrist.

"Jered, what's going on?"

"Where are you?" His voice held outrage in each tone.

I needed to think speedy. "I'm out right now, simply getting some required things."

"Truly," he was as yet infuriated. "Since I just went to your room. You never replied, and when I opened the entryway the room was unfilled."

"I moved to a superior area."

I began to recognize more easily than outrage. "What's more, you did as such without telling me? I was stressed something happened to you."

"I'm fine, Jered." I guaranteed him. "I'm on the port side of the boat, the grandiose rooms."

"OK, I'll meet you there and- - " He began.

I intruded on him. "No! Um, what about we meet at Asteroid Burger. We can talk over lunch?"

He was frightened, yet concurred. "Okay, I'll see you at thirteen ticks."

He finished the call and I inhaled a murmur of alleviation. I was unable to allow him to go to my lied home. He would realize something was up. I simply expected to ward him off and eased of stress over me. Out of everybody in the present circumstance, he was the one I needed to keep out of it most.

Jesse strolled over to me. "Goodness, I tracked down this in your stuff. I read part of it as well." His hand held my book chip of the Scarlet Pimpernel. "I think you will require a name. I additionally needed to inquire as to whether you planned to behave like this man?"

I snickered marginally. "No, I will not carry on like a Fop or a Nincompoop. I'll simply act all the more silly, what about that?"

He gestured. "Simply be cautious when you are out there. I realize Jered is your companion, yet he takes care of business for Roderick."

"I know." I checked out the time. "Twelve point eight ticks. I better go assuming I need to meet Jered on schedule. Be cautious when searching for your person."

Jesse giggled. "I will not need to stress over Bruce. He will not hurt me."

With that, we headed out in different directions for the brief time frame and went to our chose objections. I stayed calm during my excursion up to Asteroid Burger. I didn't actually have the foggiest idea what I planned to converse with Jered about, however I trusted that things would go without a hitch.

At the point when I showed up at the eatery, I saw Jered sitting tight there for me, food previously requested. I grinned and strolled towards him. When he saw me, he stood and grinned at me.

"Thank for being willing to meet with me." He began. "It's been long sufficient that I feel we want to make some corrects. What's more, I miss having you around."

"I missed you as well, Jered." I said back. "The subject of upheaval is only difficult to take in. Be that as it may, what did you need to discuss?"

We plunked down before he proceeded. "I didn't see you yesterday. I was concerned that something occurred."

I peered down. "I was there, yet I remained in the back on the grounds that you know how I feel about these things. I left straightaway."

"I needed to converse with you a piece before you left." Jered peered down at his food. "I want you to be more cautious at this point. Somebody is battling against Lord Roderick and his Revolutionaries."

My eyes enlarged. "Is that why the lights went out during the execution?"

He gestured. "This individual is battling against the unrest, and Lord Roderick has placed me accountable for finding them."

"Shouldn't something be said about that family?" I inquired.

"We've looked through the whole boat and couldn't find them. Upon additional examination we tracked down that one of the break cryo-units was absent. Which means this vigilante got them off the boat. I simply need you to be cautious." His hand covered mine.

"I can't avoid being." I guaranteed, from an alternate point of view than he had to know. "Since when have I become associated with things like this?"

"I'm not kidding, Hitomi." His hold fixed around my hand. "I'm attempting to ensure you."

I covered his hand with my own. "I know."

"My, my, who is this excellent lady?" another voice came into the discussion.

We both went aside and Jered promptly stood. "My Lord."

Oneself declared King was remaining close to us. "Goodness don't stress yourself Jered. I essentially was dropping by to perceive how you were doing, and check whether there was any advancement on the rebellious person. Yet, I should say that I am astonished to see you with such a wonderful lady." He turned towards me. "Good evening, I am Lord Roderick, however if it's not too much trouble, call me Roderick."

He knelt low and delicately kissed the rear of my hand. 'I could utilize this for my potential benefit.' I thought.

"I go by Hitomi." I bowed my head towards him. "Jered has educated me much concerning you, My Lord."

"I advised you to call me Roderick." He grinned a coquettish grin. "I feel we might have to get to know one another better. That is, in case you are free."

His eyes made a speedy look at Jered, demonstrating he was concerned that we were a couple. I grinned pleasantly at him. "Jered has been my dearest companion since I was tiny. He resembles a sibling to me."

His grinned augmented. "All things considered, then, at that point, you basically should go along with me at a Gala I will have the day after tomorrow. I couldn't want anything more than to be your escort."

"I would be regarded." I was genuinely loathing conversing with this man, however I didn't show it. "Much obliged to you, Roderick."

Jered kept quiet during our trade, yet when look and I could see he was unsettled. His had was held in a suffocating grip. His jaw was held and he was doing whatever it takes not to frown at his boss.

"Presently, Jered." Roderick went to my companion. "How are things going for you?"

"I'm fine." He began. "We are right now scanning the front port side of the Ashaton for the resistant resident. However, we have found nothing yet."

"Keep up the hunt," the King requested. "This will not be whenever they first strike. That first session was only an explanation. They will not stop at one family."

"Indeed Sir." Jered answered.

"Keep doing awesome." to Jered, he then, at that point, gone to me. "Furthermore, I will see you in two days, my dear." He kissed my hand again and went to leave.

After he had left, Jered sat down and frowned at the table. "I figured you didn't care for him."

I shrugged. "I could be off-base. He's exceptionally beguiling."

I saw his hand fixed once more. "No doubt about it."

"Its been a year." I expressed. "Individuals change, and you haven't sincerely attempted to remain associated until all the more as of late."

"It doesn't help that you essentially hindered me from your life during that year." His eyes shot up to mine. The edges of earthy colored eyes consumed gold with his outrage. He murmured. "Please accept my apologies, its been troublesome. Roderick has been riding my tail since the time this individual took that family. I suppose I'm recently drained."

"Possibly you ought to get some rest." I proposed.

"Not at the present time," he answered. "I really want to get back with the remainder of the watchman and help search."

I grinned at him. "Okay, much obliged for lunch."

Jered gave a drained grin. Standing up, he went after the hand that Roderick had kissed twice. His thumb stroked where the lord's lips contacted. He was reluctant, yet he hung over and set a little kiss on my cheek. He left without another word.

Chapter 4

I got back to my new home and found Jesse there with two others. The took a gander at me, and Jesse grinned at me. He was clearly invigorated for the news he planned to tell me.

"Hitomi," he brought me over. "This is Bruce and his significant other Rebecca. Bruce is the one I was educating you regarding before. He's incredible with instruments and apparatuses."

I strolled more than, somewhat stressed to have two additional individuals in this entire undertaking. "Jesse I thought you were simply going to contact Bruce. I would rather not put an excessive number of individuals in peril by aiding me."

"Gracious, relax." Bruce hopped in. "Becca and I are somewhat on the first spot on the list for Roderick's next kills. We both were challenging him. We as of now were at serious risk, and when we found out about what you did, we realized that we needed to join once we got the opportunity."

I actually didn't care for the possibility of a wedded couple joining. Consider the possibility that one of them passed on. "I'm not very excited with it, however you are free to remain here however long required."

"Much obliged to you." Bruce said. "In any case, I will deal with the equipment and your hardware. I will ensure that all that you use is in top execution. I previously helped Jesse fix the PC framework and get it associated with the boat centralized computer. We are on the web."

"I'll hack into Roderick's documents and frameworks so we can see who is on his rundown and begin getting those individuals to security before Roderick gets an opportunity to get them near the airtight chamber." Jesse hopped in. "It will require a day or somewhere in the vicinity before I can get in, however I will do it."

I gestured. "Before we do anything, I need to set aside effort to design things out." They concurred. "I will arrange for how and where to take these individuals so they can get off of this boat. There's few departure units with cryo-rest capacities. Yet, there's just enough for 1.3 billion individuals, the starting populace. There's as of now 1.5 billion on the Ashaton. So we want to work quick an end this transformation before we run out of these getaway units.

"Sounds like we should get all the more very close to home with Roderick." Jesse said. "Furthermore, when I say we, I mean you." He highlighted me.

"I was thinking exactly the same thing." I expressed. "It appears Roderick has an interest in me. He welcomed me to be his date at the Gala he's holding in two days."

"Would i be able to assist with your look?" Becca seized the news. "I can make you powerful."

"Becca was a cosmetologist before she and I needed to crawl under a rock." Bruce clarified. "She needed to assist you with making another outfit for when you're the Blue Rose."

"Since when was I the Blue Rose?" I inquired.

Rebecca lifted her hand marginally. "That is my issue. I saw an image of you and perceived how blue your eyes were and the name kind of recently came. I've had huge loads of thoughts for your look and I couldn't imagine anything better than to make it for you. That way you look extraordinary and say something." She took out a little book from her pocket. "I've even outlined a few thoughts of your calling card, or image."

I was intrigued at Rebecca's energy. "Okay, you can deal with my appearance for the Blue Rose. That incorporates any time I am heading off to some place with Roderick. On the off chance that I can get him so his gatekeeper is down, possibly I could end this unrest."

"However, I don't figure you should kill him." Jesse hopped in. "Consider it, Roderick most likely has someone else under him that will essentially have his spot. His right hand man would probably do it."

My heart twinged with torment. Roderick's right hand man was Jered. Would he really do that if Roderick passed on? I no longer knew who Jered was, thus I couldn't say whether I could trust him.

"Perhaps we don't have to kill anybody." Bruce noticed. "Perhaps we can find something against Roderick that would demonstrate that he isn't deserving of the title and force he wants. Show individuals who support him how off-base they are in confiding in him. Perhaps it will kick off the explanation we had a vote based system in any case."

I collapsed my arms and grinned. "That is a fantastic thought, Bruce. We can chip away at that. Jesse," I went to him. "When you are in Roderick's framework, begin searching for any data that we can use against him. Bruce, I speculate you will begin making some gear I can utilize?" He gestured. "Rebecca, accompany me and we will begin making arrangements for the Gala, hair, cosmetics, shoes, hidden weapons, everything."

We each isolated to our spaces and started to work. The time went elapsed each tick as we kept on enumerating all aspects of our arrangements. This arrangement would be unique in relation to most in light of the fact that I didn't have the foggiest idea about the design of the space the Gala would be. We didn't have the plans of the boat yet either, so we needed to anticipate a few results. The principle objective of this arrangement was to fascinate the King to be charmed by me. The nearer I could get to him, the more data I could get.

I began to get one more call as the later ticks had come. It was twenty point three ticks. Everybody went quiet as I took a gander at my wrist. It was Jered once more. I stood up and went to an alternate space for security and to shield my new companions from being seen by the skipper of the watchman.

"Hello Jered," I addressed once his 3D image showed up. "What's happening?"

"Where are you at the present moment?" He inquired.

"Simply meandering with regards to near and dear, why?"

He marked. "Would you be able to meet me at Orion park?"

He sounded tired. I gave him a little grin. "Definitely, I'll arrive in point one ticks."

"Much obliged to you," he finished the call and I began to make a beeline for the recreation center.

The Ashaton was made to make all encounters outside of a structure appear as though you were in an open air world. Set occasions and seasons happened on planned frameworks to cause it to feel like you were still on Earth. Enormous structures turned into the urban communities of the Ashaton, and the front of the boat was worked for huge ranches where food is developed and raised. With controlled conditions, food was consistently in plenitude and nobody on board would go hungry.

I came to the recreation center and thought that it is unfilled and dull because of the night sky. Checking out I looked out for my companion. What separated him more than anything else was his dull red hair. It scarcely had any orange tones to them, and it was normally that tone. In the wake of strolling around for a piece, I thought that he is perched on a seat, inclining toward his knees with his elbows, his head down.

I plunked down close to him and put a hand on his back, attempting to comfort him. He didn't move. I didn't have a clue why he was disturbed, yet I should have been there for him. After what felt like an entire tick later, he lifted one hand that held a chip.

"That is Lord Roderick's calling data." He clarified. "He needed me to get it to you."

I got it and set it in my pocket. "Is that why you're vexed?"

He didn't reply. That let me know all I had to know.

"Much thanks to you for getting it to me. I'll hit him and set up a spot and time he can get me for the Gala. Then, at that point - "

"Hitomi." Jered interfered.

I murmured and glanced over to him and froze. As I had turned he hung over and put his lips on mine. The kiss was delicate and unforeseen. I didn't realize he felt as such with regards to me. Be that as it may, for what reason would he say he was then appearance his sentiments to me? He might have let me know some other time, however why then, at that point? I was playing a risky game that could cause my passing. I would have rather not put him through that. That is the reason I was attempting to keep a superior distance between us. This kiss wasn't making a difference.

He pulled away and looking into my wide eyes. "I never considered you a sister. I simply needed you to know."

He stood up and left, his head hung low. I speculated that he felt that I wouldn't acknowledge him in case I was showing interest for a ruler. Despite the fact that I disagreed with or like Roderick. I was unable to get Jered more involved. To ensure him, I needed to allow his heart to break, which made my heart break.

Tears stung at my eyes, and I murmured an expression of remorse. "Please accept my apologies, Jered. Please accept my apologies."

Chapter 5

The day of the Gala arrived, and I was scared out of my wits. Rebecca had a wonderful dress prepared for me. She said the soft blue color made my eyes stand out. She made sure to take a lot of time to make sure I was prepared for the party. She had the most fun with my hair though. It took her three ticks just to finish it. How she styled it made it look like a fountain of ink flowing down my back. The makeup she did was simple but very effective, calling attention to my eyes and lips.

The dress was the most beautiful of the style. It was a floor length flowing dress that flared at the hips. The sweetheart cut of the neck line was lined with gems and the sleeves draped down my arms opening up at the elbow. It was the most formal of outfits I had ever warn. The shoes had the same color of the dress and were designed to look similar to Cinderella's. I just hoped that I was going to be able to stand them for a long period of time. I never was much of a high heel kind of girl.

A few point ticks before Roderick and I were to meet, I walked out to where Jesse and Bruce where. Both didn't expect my appearance. Jesse remained silent with a jaw to the ground while Bruce recovered faster and gave his wife a strong hug.

"I didn't expect any less of my wife. You have out done yourself, Becky." He kissed her cheek.

She had a wide grin. "It felt good to do what I'm good at again. But I need to also get started on the Blue Rose's uniform."

Jesse finally found a voice. "You look amazing, Hitomi. Just be careful while you are with Roderick."

I nodded. "Thanks, Jesse. I better get going." I turned to the couple. "Thank you for all of your help."

With that, I left the base and made my way up to the meeting point I had previously set up with Roderick. I stood there for only a moment before a Limvi, Limo vehicle, pulled up close by. Roderick exited the vehicle and walked over to me.

"You are breath taking, my dear." He smiled and kissed my hand. I really wished I could wash it then and there. "Please come with me. The Gala awaits."

He guided me to the Limvi and opened the door for me. Once I was comfortably in the Limvi, he entered the other side and sat next to me. He was really close to me. I didn't show him how uncomfortable I was, I needed him to think I was interested in him.

"Now my dear, Hitomi," his hand smoothed his blond hair into place. "Tell me about yourself. What do you do to keep yourself busy?"

"Oh, but Roderick," I said in a sweet voice. "I would much rather hear about you. What made you want to be king?"

"Dear, that won't work." He answered. "I wish to hear all about you, and I won't tell you a thing about me until you do."

Though I was smiling, my heart sank. This guy was smarter than I expected. "Well, I always loved history. So, most of the time I read historical book chips."

"Fascinating," he commented. "I enjoy such things as well. My favored topics are of the four world wars and their leaders."

"They are intriguing." I agreed. "But I do enjoy some historical fiction." His eyes stared into mine as he waited for me to continue. "Such as *A Tale of Two Cities*."

"And what else do you enjoy?" He asked.

I thought for a moment. "I enjoy strategic games."

"Such as Conqueror?" His back straightened.

I laughed. "No one will go against me in that game."

He smirked at me. "I see I will have to test your skills in this game. You see I am also a master of Conqueror. Maybe I will give you the challenge you need."

"That would be wonderful."

"Ah," Roderick looked out the window. "We are here. Come Hitomi."

I followed him out the door, holding his hand. The sight took my breath away. I had never been to a party such as this. There were so many people dancing and having fun.

But I was reminded that these people were the ones who sentenced innocence to the cold grip of space. I was still staring at the lights and décor of the Gala when Roderick pulled me to his side.

"What do you think, my dear?" He whispered in my ear.

A chill ran up my spine at his action. "It's beautiful, thank you for bringing me."

By being with Roderick, it caused a lot of attention on me. Many people wished to meet me and know the woman who was the king's date. I did notice how some young woman seemed to give me a hateful look, but they didn't say anything. All I needed to do right then was build a relationship with the king and earn his trust so I could get the information I needed to end this revolution.

"Hitomi?"

My heart fell to the ground. I knew that voice, and it pained me to hear it again so soon. I turned and saw the face of my best friend, Jered. He was dressed in the formal guard attire that symbolized his rank. He looked genuinely shocked. Whether it was for me being there or how I looked, I didn't know.

"Jered!" Roderick greeted with a smile. "I must say you have hidden a true beauty from me, my friend. Doesn't she look magnificent?"

"Yes sir," he said with his head down.

“I really must thank you, Jered. If it wasn’t for you I wouldn’t have met her.” Roderick grabbed my hand and placed in the crook of his arm. “Come Hitomi, we have many to still greet. And I expect several dances.”

As we walked away I heard Jered whisper to himself. “She always was beautiful.”

My heart ached a bit, but I had my job to do. Then, I had to forget about Jered and focus on Roderick. We joined another crowd and began to talk about many topics. I wasn’t there as Hitomi. I was there as the Blue Rose.

Chapter 6

I was still at the Gala, and things had calmed down to the point that I could relax a bit. One of Roderick's advisers pulled him away from me for a bit. So, I took the opportunity to step out to the garden just outside the Gala area. Distancing myself from the party allowed some silence to further relax me, and I looked up to the night sky. Being in space allowed millions to billions of stars to shine bright. I could easily make out the milky way. For the first time in a year, I felt some semblance of peace.

"Quite a view isn't it?" A voice caught me off guard. I turned to see Jered looking up to the sky as well. He had a small smile on his lips. "Reminds me of when we were in school. You would convince me to break curfew just for a bit and come out to see the stars."

I smiled at him. "If I remember correctly, you were just as excited to break curfew."

"I don't remember that." His hand raised to his chin as he thought. "I remember sleeping soundly until you practically jumped on me to wake me up."

I walked over to him. "No, you were so excited that you could hardly sleep. You were so tired the next day that you fell asleep in class."

He snapped his fingers. "Right, now I remember. The teacher got so mad that she sent me to the Dean of the school and I was going to have to take remedial courses. My parents were so mad."

I laughed. “Yeah, they placed cameras in yours and my room to make sure it didn’t happen again.”

His gaze softened. “And you were there with me the whole time. If you didn’t come and talk to the Dean with me, I don’t know what would have happened. You were always there to help me get out of trouble.”

“What are friends for?” I asked him.

We were silent for a moment. Neither of us were sure what to say next. I didn’t want things to be awkward between us. He was my best friend for a reason. We grew up together, almost like siblings. His parents were my foster parents. I never knew my parents. I was abandoned. Jered and his family became my family, and he was the best guy I could ask for while growing up. He helped me feel wanted and loved. I just never expected his feelings to be so strong.

I could feel his brown eyed gaze on me. I could tell that he had said all he needed to. He was just waiting for me to give some sort of reply. I just didn’t know what that reply was.

“I’m worried.” He broke the silence. “Roderick has not shown you his dark side yet. I have seen that side.” I looked up at him listening intently to his words. “I don’t agree with how he deals with people who disagree with him. I never thought he would take things this far on getting what he wanted. But I’m worried that he will find out that you don’t agree with his plans. I am terrified that if that happens I’ll be watching you die with reinforced glass between us. I don’t want to see that happen.”

I reached up and rested my hand on his bicep. "Don't worry, I'm being careful. And I think Roderick is too infatuated with me that he would kill me."

"That's exactly what I'm worried about." Jered responded, his brown eyes holding a sense of urgency. "He doesn't do well with people he thinks betrays him. If he falls for you and finds out that you don't support *his* revolution, he will crack and you will die."

I couldn't ignore Jered's warning. He had more time and experience around the false king. So, he knew what he was talking about. He was genuinely worried about me. After everything that happened between us, he still cared deeply for me. It warmed my heart.

He lifted his hand and softly caressed my cheek with his knuckles. "I just want you to be safe. Please, consider not seeing Roderick again."

I didn't get to answer. Roderick had found me. "There you are my dear. Come, one of my favorite songs will be playing soon and I simply must dance with you."

I stepped back from Jered and he straightened his back. Jered still was like a soldier when the king was around. It was only around me that anyone could see who he truly was.

"I'm sorry for wandering off, Roderick." I turned and smiled at him. "I just needed some air."

His hand went to the small of my back. "You are fine, dear. I'm glad that I could escape for a short time as well. Oh,

Jered" Roderick leaned closer to my friend and whispered something in his ear that I couldn't hear. But I noticed Jered's jaw tense and his hands squeeze into fists.

"Yes Sir."

"Good man. Keep me informed on the defiant." Roderick called back to him as he guided me back to the party.

One glance back, and I saw that Jered was still stiff. I wondered what Roderick had said to him. I wasn't going to find out anytime soon though.

The Gala had ended and Roderick was taking me home, at least to where he thought my home was. It was two ticks and I needed some sleep. As I thought about it, the Gala itself was fairly fun, but I would have had more fun if I wasn't with Roderick the majority of the time.

"Alright, my dear." Roderick's voice interrupted my thoughts. "Here we are. Thank you for joining me tonight. It was the best I have ever had."

I smiled at him. "It was an honor to spend this time with you, Roderick. Thank you for inviting me."

"I would like to see you again, if that is possible" He reached up and cupped my cheek in his hand. "I have never met a woman as extraordinary as you."

"You have my contact information." I flirted. "Simply call me when you want to see me."

My acting had been fairly convincing, because he took that as an invitation. Leaning closer to me, he pulled my head toward him. His lips landed on mine. But compared to Jered's, Roderick's kiss was hungrier. He was practically begging me to open my mouth.

I returned his kiss, but kept it chaste and quick. Pushing him away, I bit my lip with a smile. "Bye."

As I opened the door, he grabbed my hand. "Wait."

My finger landed on his lips, silencing him. "If you're patient, I may let you go further next time."

He smiled and laughed an excited chuckle and straightened his tie. My spine threw up a little at his action and I left the Limvi. Closing the door, I watched as it drove off, leaving me alone in the same area I had met up with him. I needed to buy some mouth wash.

By the time I had got home, half the mouth wash in the bottle was gone and I was still swishing a new mouth full round. I couldn't get rid of the gross feeling of his dry lips. Jesse walked into the room I was in. I could tell he just woke up.

Looking at the mouth wash, his tired voice asked, "He kiss you?"

I hummed a yes, trying to keep the liquid in my mouth.

His nose wrinkled and he went back into his room to sleep again. As he did that, I turned to the sink and spat out the liquid before taking another cup.

Chapter 7

The following day, Roderick called me to go along with him at the downtown area. He expected to take me out somewhere pleasant and have some alone time with me. However I feared going, Becky assisted me with sprucing up for the event and I ventured out from headquarters to go to the assigned gathering place. My heart beat once my eyes saw the despot. Putting on my cover of guiltless fascination towards the ruler, I strolled over and heard his voice direct a request.

"Incredible occupation on getting this agitator." He grinned joyously at certain troopers. "It's a disgrace your family was at that point killed before you. Yet, relax, you will go along with them soon." He turned and saw me. "Ok, my dear, I'm happy you could come so rapidly. Presently you get to see the force I have over individuals."

Pulling me over by the abdomen, he established a dry kiss on my cheek. I grinned at him and checked out the announced miscreant. My eyes enlarged briefly in shock. It was just a youngster. He was most likely between the ages of eight and ten, and he was distant from everyone else. How is it possible that Roderick would do this to an honest kid.

"Take him to my fight transport." Roderick directed. "Work him till he drains, then, at that point, continue to work him till he passes on."

My heart broke at his order. This was a youngster that would be worked to death if I sat idle. The kid was generally snatched and hauled away from where we stood. Roderick's consideration went to me.

"Please accept my apologies you needed to observe that, however you should comprehend," He held my hands in his. "I'm freeing this vessel of vermin and giving a superior everyday routine to the people who have the right to experience."

I grinned gently at him and gestured. "I comprehend. Penances should be made for a superior life."

His smile became more extensive. "I realized you would comprehend. I have an inclination you and I were bound to meet."

"I don't know much with regards to predetermination, however I am happy that I grabbed your eye. These beyond couple of days have been the most joyful of my life, realizing I would see you again soon." I ventured nearer to him and snuggled into him.

He returned my kind gestures by folding his arms over me. I pulled away before one of his hands voyaged excessively low. His grin never floundered from his elements. He caught my hand and directed me over towards Jered.

"Jered, old buddy," Roderick called to him. Jered turned and immediately noticed our held hands. Roderick couldn't see it, yet I saw that he was harmed. "Kindly consider us my Limvi, I will be taking Hitomi out for the remainder of the day."

"Indeed Sir." Jered recognized and lifted his wrist to settle on the decision.

I made a move to act. I lifted my wrist, going about as though a call was coming. "Please accept my apologies Roderick. I want to take this genuine fast."

He grinned. "Obviously, my dear. I will stand by here."

"Much thanks to you."

Strolling off a brief distance, so nobody would hear me, I called my group. "Folks, we have a circumstance."

"What's happening?" Jesse inquired.

"Roderick just sent a youngster to his conflict boat to be worked to death as a slave. I want to get him out." I clarified just.

Bruce ringed in, "It's presumably the Drogger. I dealt with that boat. I can send you a few schematics. It's most likely still on the Port side of the Ashaton. In the event that you meet Becky at the docks, she can present to you your Blue Rose uniform and supplies."

"In any case, how might you move past there?" Jesse's voice came in.

I shook my head. "I don't have the foggiest idea, however I will find a way. That kid won't pass on."

I shut the call and went to get back to Roderick. After a couple of steps, I found Jered. I was astonished to see him so out of nowhere. I grinned at him, since I was really glad to see him once more. Things without Roderick around caused it to feel more normal, more loose.

However, he was excessively unsettled. "Roderick needed me to beware of you. Is everything okay?"

I needed to consider something speedy. The hardest thing about this was that I needed to mislead both Roderick and my dearest companion to make everything reasonable. I cycle my lip and shook my head. "One more companion of mine is truly wiped out this moment and in the clinic. I want to move past there. They couldn't say whether she will make it."

His eyebrows weave together. "Who? Do I know her? Would i be able to help in any capacity?"

"She goes by Becky. No you don't have any acquaintance with her, and if I want anything I'll call you." I gave him a tragic grin. "I'll request that Roderick drop me off at the Port side clinic and hold off for while on our date."

A blaze of torment crossed Jered's eyes when I said date, yet he realized more significant issues were within reach. "Okay, we should move past to the Limvi and we will get you there at the earliest opportunity."

I gestured strolled passed Jered in an animated speed. Before I could get excessively far he snatched my hand, keeping me down a little.

"Simply be cautious OK. I realize Becky will be fine, since you will deal with her. Simply be cautious in light of the fact that there are a great deal of eyes at that emergency clinic." He clarified.

I didn't completely get what he implied, however I gestured and advanced toward Roderick. He welcomed me with a grin, however it blurred when he saw my pain. I disclosed a similar circumstance to him as I did with Jered and he took me to the medical clinic without a second thought.

"Are you certain you don't need me to come in with you?" He asked, his voice holding some worry for me.

I shook my head. "I don't need you to get the opportunity of perhaps being affected by whatever she has. You want to continue to go about your business for individuals on this boat. I'll deal with Becky."

"Okay, my dear." He pressed my hand. "Call me on the off chance that you want me."

I gestured. His hands measured my face and he pulled me over for a speedy enthusiasm filled kiss before I left the vehicle. I waved him a farewell and ran towards the medical clinic. When I was çoncealed, I made a b-line to the docks. Checking out I found Becky stowing away in a room out of the way holding a pack in her arms.

"Here is your uniform, and Bruce likewise gave a few devices to you to utilize." She disclosed as I wearing the dim uniform. "Staggering firearm and stick. Smoke pellets for interruptions. This is a hacking bracer, use it to open and locks or entryways. It will likewise interface with any PC frameworks and Jesse can associate with the frameworks. Com-connect ear piece, its generally set so you can hear us, and we will hear you and whatever is going on around you. Furthermore, your calling card."

"Calling card?" I turned at checked out the hand held gadget.

"Bruce and Jesse came to show the plan of your image. It's an arrangement of lasers that consume into metal, leaving a blue gleaming shade. This way individuals know who there is a saint saving lives. It will give them trust."

I got done with dressing and put the things in the many pockets and cases on my jeans and belt. Rebecca truly did something extraordinary for herself in this uniform. It was dark in a unique way of blue along the creases. My Jacket had a corner to corner zipper that opened up to a defensively covered shirt holding a similar image of the Blue Rose as my calling card. The protective layer reached out up my neck and turned into a half facial covering my nose and mouth. My hair was pulled up in a high pig tail. I wore knee high wedged boots that held my immobilizer in one and my paralyze stick in the other. I felt prepared.

Becky proceeded, "The material of your suit is made with the solid microfibers imbued with steel. Laser Blasts will not effectively get past. Your bracers can redirect lasers, so utilize those to obstruct."

I noticed how the two bracers been able to reflect like a mirror, and I got why. The dim metal on my wrists mirrored my blue eyes. This was my first time going into something on the fly with no earlier arranging. I realized I must have the option to anticipate the spot. That implied requiring some investment to investigate my environmental elements and thinking quick.

"In this way, how are you going to get on?" Becky posed the inquiry everybody was pondering, even me.

I checked out the corner and looked as a flimsy man ventured off a boat and started strolling thusly. "Him. He will get me on. Return to base, I'll be in touch."

She gestured and ran off into the shadows, advancing toward headquarters inconspicuous. I remained where I was and observed quietly as this man continued strolling towards my concealing region. I came to down and snatched the daze stick and held it in a converse grasp. When he was in reach, I got his collar and pulled him in. I didn't need any other person engaged with this, yet when all else fails, compromise is unavoidable. I pushed him against the divider and held the adhere to his neck.

"All things considered, this is a shock," he expressed in a smooth voice. "Relatively few ladies are the ones maneuvering me into an isolated region."

"Calm, or you will be taken out quicker that you can yell for help." I frowned at him. "I really want you to get me onto that boat." I pointed at the Drogger.

Loose, his eyes followed my weapon and checked out the huge fight transport. "You do understand that that is a conflict transport? Which means there are a great deal of weapons and individuals who will kill the people who are approved to be on there."

"I know, however there is a young man on that transport who is likely being beaten and worked to death since his family conflicted with Roderick. I really want to get on there and save him." My glare proceeded.

"Never preferred Roderick, or his associates." His eyes remained on the boat. He let out a drained moan and his head dropped down prior to glancing back at me. "Okay, I'll get you on, however you must compensation me fifteen thousand in Yellows."

__THE END__

www.ingramcontent.com/pod-product-compliance
Lightning Source LLC
LaVergne TN
LVHW050347160826
845677LV00014B/3846